Ghouls Don't Scoop Ice Cream

There are more books about the Bailey School Kids!
Have you read these adventures?

Ghouls Don't Scoop Ice Cream

by Debbie Dadey
and
Marcia Thornton Jones

illustrated by John Steven Gurney

A
LITTLE APPLE
PAPERBACK

SCHOLASTIC INC.
New York   Toronto   London   Auckland   Sydney

No part of this publication may be reproduced in whole or in part, or stored in a retrieval system, or transmitted in any form or by any means, electronic, mechanical, photocopying, recording, or otherwise, without written permission of the publisher. For information regarding permission, write to Scholastic Inc., Attention: Permissions Department, 555 Broadway, New York, NY 10012.

ISBN 0-590-25819-2

12 11 10 9 8 7 6 5 4 3 2 1   8 9/9 0 1 2 3/0

Printed in the U.S.A.   40

First Scholastic printing, May 1998

For all the "ghouls" and "boos" in the

schools where I teach!—MTJ

For Damon Gibson—a great nephew—DD

Contents

Ghouls Don't Scoop Ice Cream

1

Vampire Teacher

"I can't believe it," Eddie complained after school.

Melody sat down hard on the ground under the big oak tree beside her friends Eddie, Howie, and Liza. Melody's black pigtails bounced as she shook her head. "I can't believe we have to do one hundred math problems before tomorrow."

"I wanted to finish reading my library book." Liza looked ready to cry. "Now I have to spend the whole night figuring out these problems."

Howie opened his math book to page ninety-six. "Actually, these review problems are very easy. It'll be fun."

Eddie threw his baseball cap at Howie. "Math is not fun. Soccer is fun. A Doo-

dlegum Shake is fun, but math is not fun!"

"Doodlegum Shakes!" Liza shrieked. "That'll make us feel better. Let's go get one." The four kids took off across the playground. They looked both ways before crossing Forest Lane and racing down the sidewalk to Burger Doodle Restaurant.

"I bet the other third-graders don't have to do all those math problems," Eddie complained.

"That's because other third-graders don't have a vampire for a teacher," Howie said.

"We never actually proved that Mrs. Jeepers is a vampire," Liza said when they turned the corner. "After all, if she was a real vampire then how could she be awake during the day? Vampires are supposed to be awake only at night."

"It's because of her magic brooch," Eddie told her. "I bet that's the reason she can be awake during the day."

Liza put her hands on her hips as they stood in front of Burger Doodle Restaurant. "Even if she is a vampire, maybe she can't help herself."

Howie closed his math book. "Maybe Mrs. Jeepers isn't a vampire. Maybe she's a ghoul."

"A ghoul!" Eddie and Liza shouted together.

"What in the world is a ghoul?" Liza asked.

"A ghoul is a spy for a vampire," Howie explained. "I learned about ghouls when I was reading a book about vampires."

Melody nodded. She remembered when Howie and she had read that garlic would repel vampires. They had taken a bottle of garlic salt and sprinkled it around their classroom. Sure enough, their teacher, Mrs. Jeepers, had started sneezing. She was allergic to the garlic, just like a vampire.

Liza grabbed the door handle to Burger Doodle. "Let's forget all this crazy talk

4

about ghouls and vampires and get a big, fat Doodlegum Shake."

"All right!" Eddie yelled and barged past Liza. But what he saw inside the restaurant made him stop dead in his tracks.

2

Scout

"Who is that?" Melody whispered, pointing to the figure behind the Burger Doodle counter.

"She's the new counter worker," Howie explained.

"How can you tell it's a she?" Eddie asked. "I can't even see her face." It was true. The new worker wore a dark blue sweat suit with the hood pulled up over her head.

"My dad brought me here last night," Howie told them. "When you get up close, she looks like a girl."

"Come on," Liza said. "Let's get our shakes." Liza walked right up to the counter. "One Doodlegum Shake, please," she said.

The girl behind the counter looked up

with red eyes that seemed to stare right through Liza. The counter girl didn't smile, and she was so pale, she looked sick. Silently, she made the shake with slow movements, then sat it in front of Liza. "That will be one dollar," the girl said. It sounded like she was talking in her sleep.

Liza gulped and pulled a dollar out of her jacket pocket. When Liza handed over the money, she noticed the girl's name tag. It said SCOUT in big white letters.

Liza took the shake to a far corner booth and waited for her friends. When they arrived with their shakes, they spoke in hushed tones.

"Did you see that girl's eyes?" Eddie asked. "I think she was up all night milking the cow to make these milk shakes."

"Shhh," Liza said. "Maybe she's sick and she can't help how her eyes look."

"If she's sick," Eddie said loudly, "she should be at home in bed, not making my milk shakes. I don't want to end up with red eyes, too."

Melody giggled. "Red eyes would match your red hair perfectly."

"And Scout's syrup," Howie said, nodding toward the counter.

The kids stared at Scout. The hooded girl silently scooped a big blob of red ice cream into a dish and then poured a heavy red liquid on top. Scout took the dish to a small table in the back where

she stuck her pale face close to the dish and started slurping.

"Yuck," Melody said softly. "Doesn't she have any manners?"

Liza nervously took a sip of her milk shake and continued watching Scout lick up the red syrup. When she finished, the new counter girl looked up with her red eyes. Liza choked on her milk shake when she noticed how the sticky red syrup dribbling down Scout's chin looked just like blood.

3

Neighborhood of the Dead

The bells on the door of Burger Doodle jingled when it opened suddenly. Eddie quickly lowered his head and slurped his shake. He wasn't fast enough to miss Carey batting her long eyelashes in his direction. Carey was in their class, and she had a habit of following Eddie wherever he went.

Melody giggled. "Carey likes you," she told Eddie.

"She does not," Eddie said.

"Then why does she always wink at you?" Liza asked.

"Because she's batty," Eddie said. "Ignore her so she'll go away."

Carey didn't go away. Instead, she skipped across the floor so that her blond curls bounced. She stopped right by

Eddie. "I knew I'd find you here," Carey said. "I think I'll get a shake, too!"

"I'd like to shake her," Eddie mumbled when she skipped to the counter. "I'd shake her all the way to the North Pole."

"Be nice," Liza warned. "She isn't hurting anyone."

"Not yet," Eddie said as Carey brought her drink to their table and squeezed in between Eddie and Melody.

"Why aren't you home working on the math problems?" Howie asked.

Carey shook her head and batted her eyelashes. "I can't go home yet. We're moving today. My daddy just bought a house on Olympus Lane."

Carey's father was the president of the Bailey City Bank. Her family had more money than anyone in Bailey City. Carey was used to getting everything she wanted.

Carey spoke loudly enough for everyone in the entire restaurant to hear. "Our house is the biggest one in the entire neighborhood."

Melody rolled her eyes. "It may be the biggest, but I wouldn't want to live there," she told Carey.

"Why not?" Carey asked.

"Because," Melody said, "all those houses are next to the cemetery. It's the neighborhood of the dead!"

Eddie started to laugh, but just then Scout's ice cream scooper clattered to the floor. Liza gasped when Scout headed their way. She was moving so fast over the shiny linoleum that it looked like she was gliding.

The five kids looked up into the red eyes of the strange ice cream worker. Scout stared straight at Carey. "Tell me all about your new neighborhood," Scout asked in her slow, serious voice.

"There are not many houses," Carey told her. "It is very quiet, especially since the cemetery is close by."

Eddie laughed. "That's right," he said. "There's no one to bother you except dead people."

"Excellent," Scout said slowly.

"Why do you want to know about Carey's neighborhood?" Liza asked.

Scout turned her red eyes toward Liza. "Because," she said, "the family I work for is planning to move to Bailey City. I came before them to . . . investigate."

"Investigate what?" Howie asked.

"I am looking for the perfect house," Scout said. "And I think I might find it in Carey's neighborhood!"

Scout slowly turned and made her way back to the ice cream counter. The five kids watched her grab a small tape recorder. Scout talked in low tones into the tiny recorder.

"That girl gives me the creeps," Melody said.

"I've never heard of a house detective before," Eddie said.

Howie shook his head. "I don't think she's a detective," he said. "I think she's a spy!"

4

Bailey City Spy

The next morning Liza, Howie, Eddie, and Melody met under the giant oak tree on the Bailey School playground.

"I stayed up an hour past my bedtime and I still didn't finish all my homework," Liza complained.

Howie shrugged. "It wasn't that hard. Maybe I could help you."

"What homework?" Eddie asked.

"Eddie," Liza scolded, "you'll never get out of third grade if you don't do your homework."

"That means you'll be stuck with a vampire teacher for the rest of your life!" Melody warned him. She pointed across the playground to Mrs. Jeepers, who was walking toward the school.

Mrs. Jeepers wore a polka-dotted dress

and had long red hair. The sun glinted off the green pin she always wore at her throat. It was the brooch most kids were sure was magic.

"Mrs. Jeepers doesn't scare me," Liza said, "but that new ice cream worker at Burger Doodle does! It's creepy having a spy in Bailey City."

"Scout is not a spy," Eddie said. "After all, there isn't much to spy on around here."

"Maybe she's here to meet up with another spy," Howie said slowly.

"What are you talking about?" Melody asked. "There aren't any Bailey City spies."

"Then why is Mrs. Jeepers talking into a tape recorder, too?" Liza asked. Liza pointed across the playground. Mrs. Jeepers had stopped in the shadows of the school building. She stared at the four friends under the oak tree, and she talked into a tape recorder that looked exactly like the one Scout had used the night before.

"You can't believe Mrs. Jeepers is a spy, too," Melody said. "Teachers are too busy grading math papers to spy."

"It is strange that her tape recorder is exactly like Scout's," Liza told them.

Eddie interrupted his friends. "Just a minute," he said. "My shoe is ringing." He slipped off his shoe and held it up to Liza's ear. "It's the super-spy channel for

Liza. They want to know what it's like to have a head full of air."

Liza batted away Eddie's stinky sneaker. "Make jokes if you want to," Liza said. "But I think there is something strange happening in Bailey City."

"Tell her she's being silly," Melody said to Howie.

Howie didn't say a word. His face was white and his hands shook as he hurried to pull out a book from his backpack.

"I do have something to say," Howie told his friends. "But I have a feeling you're not going to like it!"

5

Spies for the Living Dead

"You're absolutely right," Eddie said. "I don't want to hear anything except my foot kicking a soccer ball!"

"You won't be hearing that after school," Melody warned, "because you have to stay after to finish your math homework."

"No way," Eddie grumbled. "I plan to get another Doodlegum Shake after school."

Howie shook his head. "You might change your mind when you hear what I found out when I was researching," he told Eddie.

"Let me guess," Eddie said. "You found out there's something scary about kids who do research for fun?"

"No," Howie said.

22

GET CREEPY WITH THE BAILEY SCHOOL KIDS CLUB!
FREE! GLOW-IN-THE-DARK MONSTER NAILS!

MAGAZINE
THE BAILEY SCHOOL KIDS MAGAZINE
The Real Scoop On Gargoyles
A Hunchback of Notre Dame Poster!

OFFICIAL MONSTER PACK $2.95 PLUS SHIPPING AND HANDLING

The Adventures of THE BAILEY SCHOOL KIDS
Gargoyles Don't Drive School Buses
Who is this strange new driver?
by Debbie Dadey and Marcia Thornton Jones

#11
The Adventures of THE BAILEY SCHOOL KIDS
Skeletons Don't Play Tubas
Band class can be bone chilling!
2 BOOKS
by Debbie Dadey and Marcia Thornton Jones

MEMBERSHIP CARD

JOKE BOOK
The Adventures of THE BAILEY SCHOOL KIDS
The Bailey School Kids Joke Book

◄ DETACH ►

POSTER
The Adventures of THE BAILEY SCHOOL KIDS CLUB
WATCH OUT! There are some pretty weird grown-ups in Bailey city...

BOOKENDS

□ **YES, please enroll me in The Adventures of the Bailey School Kids Club** (8Y3K1B)

Send my introductory 8-piece monster pack for the introductory offer price of $2.95 (plus shipping and handling). Then every month, for as long as I like, I will continue to receive new packs—each with two more Bailey School Kids books, the next Bailey School Kids magazine and a monster-ous activity—for just $7.95 (plus shipping and handling and applicable sales tax). I may cancel at any time.

□ Boy □ Girl   Mo_____Day_____Year_____ _____
Birthday   Grade

_____
First Name   Last Name

_____
Address   (print in ink)

_____
City   State   Zip

(_____) _____
Telephone Number

_____
Parent's Signature (must be signed)

Offer valid in U.S. zip-coded address only. Limit one per child.

The Adventures of THE BAILEY SCHOOL KIDS

GET CREEPY WITH THE BAILEY SCHOOL KIDS CLUB!

FREE! GLOW-IN-THE-DARK MONSTER NAILS!

Your Official Monster Pack includes:

- *Gargoyles Don't Drive School Buses*
- *Skeletons Don't Play Tubas*
- *The Bailey School Kids Joke Book*

- The Bailey School Kids Magazine
- Bailey School Kids Bookends
- Mysterious Membership Card
- Monster-ous Poster *Plus...*

- **FIVE GLOW-IN-THE-DARK MONSTER NAILS FREE!**

BAILEY SCHOOL KIDS CLUB
SCHOLASTIC INC.
P.O. BOX 5014
CLIFTON, NJ 07015-9592

POSTAGE WILL BE PAID BY ADDRESSEE

FIRST-CLASS MAIL   PERMIT NO. 670   CLIFTON, NJ

BUSINESS REPLY MAIL

NO POSTAGE
NECESSARY
IF MAILED
IN THE
UNITED STATES

Join today!

This introductory pack will arrive at your home 4-6 weeks after you fill out and mail the attached order card. Don't forget to get your parent's signature.

Great Savings!

For as long as you like you will continue to receive new packs—each with two more Bailey School Kids books, the next Bailey School Kids magazine and a monsterous activity—for just $7.95 (plus shipping and handling). You can cancel at any time.

No risk...

To enjoy this gift-packed, free trial invitation, simply detach, complete with parent's signature, and return the postage-paid, FREE Trial Invitation form on the other side.

Respond today!

Offer expires December 31, 1998

"Then you're not as smart as I thought you were." Eddie laughed. "Everybody knows normal kids don't do research unless they have to."

"Well," Howie told Eddie, "I had to because it was a matter of life and death!"

"Since when is research a matter of life and death?" Melody asked.

"Since Mrs. Jeepers became our teacher," Howie told her. "I was trying to find out about vampires when I stumbled across something. It's right here in this book."

Howie held up his heavy book with a tattered cover. He opened the book to a bookmark. Then he read in a voice so low his friends had to crowd close just to hear.

"In the world of the undead," Howie read, "vampires depend on help from ghouls to survive. Half dead and half living, ghouls travel the earth searching for perfect homes where families of vampires can live safely. The ghouls' lives are

full of sorrow and they are rarely known to smile. Without these trustworthy spies, vampires would be in serious danger."

Howie stopped reading and looked each of his friends in the eyes. "Doesn't this prove it?" he asked.

"It proves your brain turned into a banana split," Eddie kidded.

"Eddie's right," Melody said. "What does any of this have to do with us?"

"Weren't you listening?" Howie said. "Scout said she's looking for the perfect house for a family."

Just then Liza screamed. "Oh, my gosh," she said. "You're telling us that Scout is a vampire-spying ghoul!"

6

Easter Bunny

"A spy for Mrs. Jeepers?" Melody asked.

"Sure," Eddie teased. "Scout is a spy for Mrs. Jeepers and I'm little bunny foo-foo!"

Melody giggled. "I guess that makes Liza the Easter Bunny."

"No," Eddie said. "That makes Liza crazy."

Howie slammed his book shut. "I think Liza makes perfect sense."

"It may make perfect sense if you're a jelly bean, but not if you're a normal everyday kid," Eddie argued. "Every time anyone is just a little bit different, you guys turn them into a monster."

Melody shook her head. "If that were true we would have put you in a cage a long time ago."

"Ha, ha," Eddie sneered. "The fact remains that Scout is just a strange ice cream worker, not a ghoul."

"Are you willing to bet your life on that?" Liza asked.

"Sure," Eddie said. "Why not?"

"Then let's go back to Burger Doodle after school and we'll see what we can find out about Scout," Liza said.

"All right," Eddie said. "You're on."

After school the kids ordered more Doodlegum Shakes at Burger Doodle. Scout made them their shakes, but she never smiled at them. Just like the first time, Scout made a sundae for herself, complete with a bloodred topping. She slurped it up, dribbling red liquid down her chin.

"Let's get this over with," Eddie griped. "I want to play."

"What about our spelling homework?" Howie asked. "Shouldn't you do that first?"

"I should," Eddie said with a smile, "but I'm not going to."

Liza rolled her eyes and took a sip of her shake. Eddie made a loud slurping noise as he drained his cup dry. Then he burped and folded his arms in front of his chest.

"That's gross," Liza told him.

Eddie pointed to Scout. "I'm not half as gross as her." The kids looked at Scout.

Her bowl covered her face and she licked it with her tongue to get the last of the red topping.

"I wonder what that red stuff is," Melody said.

"Haven't you people ever heard of strawberry syrup?" Eddie asked.

Liza frowned. "That doesn't look like strawberry syrup to me."

"But," Howie said, pointing out the window, "that definitely looks like trouble."

7

Batty Family

The kids pressed their noses against the window. Mrs. Jeepers was headed straight toward them, and she wasn't smiling.

"Let's get out of here," Liza squealed. "She's probably going to get us because we're not working on our spelling."

"She's already to the door," Howie said.

"There's got to be a back door out of here," Melody suggested.

Eddie nodded. "It's right behind Scout."

"Oh, no," Liza moaned. "We're trapped."

"There's only one thing to do," Melody said, grabbing her backpack.

"What?" Howie asked.

"Spelling," Melody said, pulling her

spelling book out of her backpack and opening it.

"I knew I should have played soccer," Eddie said, but he pulled his spelling book out along with Howie and Liza. All four kids had their noses in their books when Mrs. Jeepers swept into the restaurant.

Mrs. Jeepers didn't even look at the kids. She rushed over to Scout and handed her a small green notebook. Scout stared straight ahead, not even smiling. Then, without a sound, Mrs. Jeepers quickly turned and hurried out the door.

"Thank goodness," Eddie said. "I only had to answer one question."

"That was strange," Melody said. "Mrs. Jeepers acted like we weren't even here."

"She must have been in a hurry," Liza said.

"Don't you think it's strange that Mrs. Jeepers knows Scout?" Howie asked.

"We live in a city the size of a shoe box," Eddie said, smashing his cup with

31

his fist. "Why wouldn't Mrs. Jeepers know Scout?"

Howie ignored Eddie. "Maybe Mrs. Jeepers knows Scout because Scout is her spy."

"Mrs. Jeepers doesn't need a spy," Melody said. "She already knows everything about Bailey City."

"Scout said she works for a family," Liza said with a gulp. "Maybe it's a whole family of vampires."

Eddie laughed and tossed his cup toward the trash can. It sailed in without even touching the rim. "All right!" Eddie cheered. "Two points!" Then he looked at Liza. "Don't tell me you think a whole batty family is going to swoop into Bailey City as soon as a ghoulish spy finds them a nest."

"That's it!" Howie shouted. "Mrs. Jeepers is bringing more vampires to Bailey City."

Eddie rolled his eyes. "That's a bunch

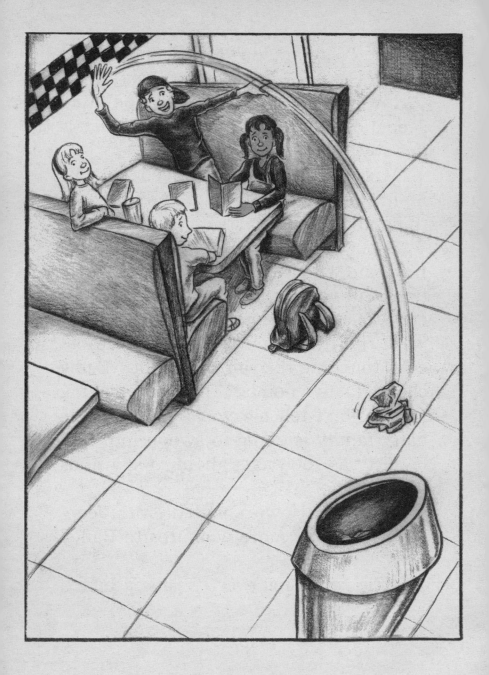

of bat poop. After all, ghouls don't scoop ice cream."

"Or do they?" Liza said, staring at Scout.

8

Drinking Blood

"I'll find out if she's really a ghoul," Eddie said, jumping up from his chair. Scout walked into the back room and Eddie headed straight to the ice cream counter.

Melody grabbed his arm. "What are you going to do?" she asked.

"I'm going to drink some of that strawberry syrup," Eddie said. "Then I'll know for sure that Scout's only a weirdo, and not a ghoul."

Liza gasped. "What if it's not strawberry syrup?" she whispered, nervously looking to see if Scout had come out yet. "What if it's blood?"

"Yuck!" Melody said. "You'd be drinking real blood."

Eddie's face went a little pale, but he

acted tough. "So what?" he said. "My dad had a drink one time called a Bloody Mary. I'll just have a Bloody Scout."

"A Bloody Mary is made from tomato juice," Howie explained. "It's not made from real blood."

Eddie rolled his eyes. "I knew that," he said. "I was just kidding around."

"Scout will be back any minute," Liza hissed. "Please sit down."

Eddie shook his head. "I've done enough sitting. It's time for action."

Eddie ran over to the counter and slid behind it. He had a big spoon in his hand when Scout came out.

"What are you doing?" Scout asked. Her pale skin and red eyes made Eddie wish he'd never heard of ghouls. Eddie was scared, but he never let on.

"I wanted to ask you a question," Eddie said.

Liza slid down in her seat and closed her eyes. "Oh, no. We're dead. He's going to ask her if she's a ghoul."

Melody squeezed her cup and shook her head. "No, Eddie's not that crazy."

"Yes, he is," Howie said sadly.

"Let's get out of here before it's too late," Liza said. She ran up to Eddie and pulled his arm. "Come on," she said. "We have to go."

"Not yet," Eddie said firmly.

"Come on," Melody said. Melody, Howie, and Liza all grabbed Eddie and started pulling.

Eddie jerked his arms away and faced Scout. Her red eyes beamed down on him from behind her dark blue hood and her tape recorder hung from the belt of her sweat suit. "What's the name of the family you work for?"

Scout touched the tape recorder at her belt. "It is a secret," she said in her hollow voice.

Eddie tried another question. "What kind of house do they want?"

"A stone dwelling with no windows and no neighbors," Scout said.

"Like a cave?" Melody blurted out.

Scout's red eyes seemed to glow as she stared at Melody. "Exactly," she said. But she didn't smile when she said it.

"That sounds like Ruby Cave," Eddie said without thinking.

Ruby Cave cut deep into nearby Ruby Mountain. Few people were brave enough to explore its many caverns, but Eddie had always wanted to try.

"Shhh," Liza said and slapped her hand over Eddie's mouth.

Scout reached toward Eddie, but Liza didn't give her a chance to get him. This time she pulled Eddie, and she pulled him hard. "Run!" she screamed.

9

Ghoul Fools

The four friends didn't slow down until they reached the cemetery.

"I can't run another step," Liza panted.

"I think we're safe now," Melody said.

Eddie kicked at the iron fence surrounding the cemetery. "I don't understand why we were running in the first place," he said.

"We were saving you from Scout," Liza told Eddie.

Eddie laughed. "All I did was ask Scout what kind of house she was looking for. I don't think that's against the law."

"Not normal Bailey City laws," Howie said. "But I have a feeling ghouls have a different set of rules."

"We have a bigger problem than ghouls in Bailey City," Eddie said seriously.

"What could be worse than ghouls?" Liza whimpered.

Eddie pointed at his friends and grinned. "Ghoul fools!" he said with a laugh.

"Vampire spies are not something to laugh about," Howie warned.

Melody nodded. "When you told Scout about Ruby Cave, she looked like she was ready to use your head as a building block," she said. "We had to save you."

"The only thing you saved me from was death by shaking." Eddie laughed. "A Doodlegum Shake!"

"Eddie's head is as thick as a brick," Liza said, "because he doesn't get any of this."

"Mrs. Jeepers' batty relatives have sent their ghoul to search Bailey City for the perfect bat cave," Howie explained to Eddie. "Her name is Scout, and she thinks you know exactly where that perfect vampire home is. She'll hunt you down to make you tell her about Ruby Cave."

"Ruby Cave isn't a secret," Eddie argued loudly. "And I'm not afraid of ghouls, fools, or vampires."

Liza slapped her hand over his mouth before he could yell any more. "I'm sure Scout would be delighted to make you her afternoon snack," she told Eddie. "But we can't let her do that."

Eddie jerked away from Liza's hand.

"Nothing could make Scout happy," Eddie said.

Liza nodded. "I've never seen a sadder person in my whole life. I guess being a ghoul is lonely."

"I'll tell you what's sad," Eddie joked. "Bailey School kids who run away, leaving perfectly delicious Doodlegum Shakes melting on the tables."

"You shouldn't make fun," Melody told Eddie. "It's no fun being sad and lonely."

Eddie rolled his eyes. "It's no fun being surrounded by crazy kids, either. But I don't see anybody feeling sorry for me!"

"You've been grinning and laughing since you were born," Liza pointed out. "Scout hasn't cracked a single smile since we met her."

Melody poked Eddie in the stomach. "Maybe it's Eddie's fault. Adults never smile when he's around." Eddie was good at causing trouble, and everybody knew it. Especially adults.

Liza giggled, but Howie didn't even smile. Instead, he slapped Eddie on the back. "That's it!" he said. "You've given me the perfect idea!"

10

Operation Eddie

Howie didn't wait for his friends. Instead, he marched back down the sidewalk. Eddie, Melody, and Liza had to hurry to catch up.

"Wait a minute," Melody said. "You're going the wrong way."

Liza grabbed Howie's arm. "We don't want to go back. Scout will get Eddie."

Howie shook his head. "We have to go back," he said. "Before it's too late!"

"It's already too late," Eddie said. "Your Doodlegum Shakes have melted to nothing but milk mush by now."

"I'm not talking about milk shakes," Howie said. "I'm talking about saving Bailey City."

"What can we do?" Liza asked. "Scout is a powerful ghoul."

48

"If what you think is true," Melody added, "then we should be running the other way. There's nothing four normal kids can do to scare away a vampire spy."

"You're right," Howie said.

"We are?" Liza said in a squeaky voice.

Howie nodded. "Absolutely. That's why this situation calls for Operation Eddie."

It was a well-known fact that Howie wanted to be a doctor when he grew up, and Eddie was sure Howie was ready to start practicing on him. Eddie took a giant step back. "I don't care if you are the smartest kid in Bailey City," Eddie yelled. "I'm not going to let you cut me open!"

"I'm not going to lay a finger on you," Howie said. "In fact, I'm not going to do anything."

"You're not making any sense," Melody complained. "First you say you're ready to battle a ghoul, then you act like you're

going to sit down and pick dandelions. What's it going to be?"

"Both," Howie said. "First, I'm going to help Eddie battle the ghoul. Then, I'm going to sit and watch."

"Now wait a minute," Eddie argued. "I don't even believe in all this ghoul stuff. Why should I have to do the dirty work?"

"Because," Howie explained, "you came up with the idea."

Eddie stood up tall and stuck out his chest. "I *am* smart," he admitted.

"Then tell us your idea," Liza begged.

Eddie slumped down as if he were a balloon that was just popped. "I'm not exactly sure," he said.

Melody laughed. "Eddie is about as smart as a turnip," she said.

"Eddie *is* smart," Howie said. "A smart aleck!"

Eddie curled his fingers into a fist. "Hey, wait a minute," he said. "You shouldn't call me names."

Howie held up his hand. "Don't go getting your shoelaces tied in knots. I'm *glad* you're funny."

"You are?" Liza asked.

Howie nodded. "Thanks to Eddie," he said, "we're going to save Bailey City!"

11

Gloom and Doom

"Will you please tell me what you're talking about!" Eddie shouted.

"Shhh," Liza said, looking at the cemetery. "Someone will hear you."

Eddie rolled his eyes. "I could yell all day and still not bother anyone in this cemetery."

Liza giggled. "I know, but it doesn't seem right to yell surrounded by graves."

"If you ask me, it's not right to tease your friends," Eddie said to Howie. "Exactly how am I supposed to save Bailey City?"

Melody and Liza put their hands on their hips and looked at Howie. "Yeah," Melody said. "What do you have in mind?"

Howie peeked over his shoulder to make sure nobody else was around. All

he saw were stone grave markers and a few birds pecking at the grass.

"Ghouls like gloom and doom," Howie told his friends. "They don't like laughter and they definitely don't like anything funny."

"You mean like Eddie?" Melody asked.

"Exactly," Howie said.

"Maybe that's why she tried to grab him," Liza said.

"She tried to grab him because he knew about Ruby Cave," Howie said. "I don't think she'll leave him alone until she knows all about the cave so her family can move here."

"I don't want some strange ice cream girl bothering me," Eddie said with a frown.

"Then listen to me," Howie said, "and all our problems will be solved." Howie whispered his plan to his friends.

Eddie shook his head several times and said, "It'll never work."

Howie pointed at Eddie. "It has to

work. Now, let's get ready. We'll meet back at Burger Doodle in exactly thirty minutes. Hurry!"

The kids rushed home to get their supplies and in exactly thirty minutes Liza, Melody, and Howie stood outside Burger Doodle. Each one was wearing a strange outfit. Melody had a huge red nose and orange shoes. She also wore her dad's big shirt.

An enormous orange tie hung around Liza's neck and she wore a straw hat that had rubber chickens sitting on top. She also carried a plastic chicken that didn't have any feathers.

Howie had his clothes on inside out and he wore black plastic glasses with a funny nose and mustache attached.

"Where's Eddie?" Melody asked.

"He'd better hurry," Liza said. "We can't do this without him."

Howie nodded toward the door. "I think we're going to have to," he said as Scout pulled open the restaurant door.

Scout did not smile when the kids walked in. "Come in," she said in her flat, deep voice. "Would you like another shake?"

Melody gulped, took a deep breath, and started singing. "Shake, shake, shake. Shake it and bake it! Shake, shake, shake, but baby don't break it!"

Howie and Liza danced inside the building with Melody. They sang and danced around the inside of the restaurant. Scout stared at them, but she never cracked a smile.

"It's not working," Liza moaned.

"Try harder," Melody said.

"SHAKE, SHAKE, SHAKE. SHAKE IT AND BAKE IT!" The kids danced around like floppy dolls and Liza whopped Howie with her dead chicken.

Still, Scout didn't smile, but she did get closer. Closer and closer she came. Finally, she grabbed Howie's arm.

"Oh, no," Liza cried. "We're dead!"

12

Super Eddie

The door flew open and in jumped Eddie. "It's Super Eddie!" he screamed. Howie, Scout, Liza, and Melody stared at Eddie. He was naked. Well, almost naked. He had on only a pair of red polka-dotted swimming trunks and a red towel pinned around his neck. On his chest a red *S* was drawn with lipstick. He had outlined his lips with the red lipstick and had blue eye shadow over his eyes.

Liza giggled and Melody cracked up. "Eddie," Howie said with a laugh, "you look ridiculous."

Eddie nodded, showing the pink flower he had stuck on top of his head. "Wasn't that the idea?" Eddie asked.

"Only it's not working," Liza said.

Eddie didn't pay any attention to Liza.

He jumped on top of the nearest table, did a little dance in his big house slippers, and then pointed at Scout.

"Have you heard the joke about the zombie's grave?" Eddie asked.

Scout slowly shook her head.

"Oh, never mind," Eddie said. "You wouldn't *dig* it anyway."

Liza giggled, but Scout only stared. Eddie tried again. "What is red, creepy, and has a red nose?" Eddie asked.

Scout shrugged. Eddie jumped off the table in front of Scout. "Rudolph, the Red-Nosed Zombie!" Eddie shouted.

"What's a ghost's favorite ice cream flavor?" Eddie asked, dancing around behind the ice cream counter.

Scout followed Eddie and shrugged her shoulders. Eddie smiled before shouting, "Boo-berry! And now, it's time we all had some." Eddie grabbed the chocolate syrup and held it over his head. Unfortunately, the ladle slipped and the chocolate syrup dumped on his head. Before Scout could move, Eddie had the whipped cream hose. Eddie pushed the wrong button and the hose squirted. He fired the whipped cream like a bazooka. *Whoosh! Whoosh!*

Liza got creamed. Melody got creamed. Howie got creamed. They all screamed and laughed. Finally, Eddie turned the hose on Scout and creamed her.

Whoosh! Cream splattered her from her head to her toes. "How about some syrup?" Eddie asked, before dumping red syrup on Scout's head.

Scout wiped her face and stared at Eddie. He had chocolate dripping down his head onto his bare chest and whipped cream on his face like a weird mustache.

The corners of Scout's mouth twitched, then turned up. Then she giggled along with Liza, Melody, and Howie.

"What's long, orange, and wears diapers?" Eddie asked.

Everyone was giggling, so Eddie an-

swered himself. "A baby carrot!" he yelled before filling his mouth with whipped cream. Then he used his hands to slap his cheeks. Whipped cream squirted everywhere just as the outside door opened. Mrs. Jeepers walked inside in time to get her face splattered with whipped cream.

When Scout took one look at Mrs. Jeepers, Scout doubled over and laughed.

The next day the kids peeked inside Burger Doodle. A teenager with pimples on his face busily wiped the counter. "I thought Mrs. Jeepers would kill you yesterday," Liza whispered to Eddie.

"I didn't mean to squirt her. I guess I got a little carried away," Eddie said. "It was an accident."

"You got a lot carried away," Liza told Eddie. "I thought we'd never get all the mess cleaned up."

"At least everything turned out all right," Melody said. "It's a good thing Mrs. Jeepers likes whipped cream."

Liza nodded. "Howie's plan worked, thanks to Eddie's silliness."

"I knew it would work," Howie said. "Laughter is the best medicine when it comes to curing a ghoul."

Melody put her hands on her hips. "How did you know it would work?" she asked.

Howie grinned. "Don't you know how to get rid of a blue monster?" he asked.

His three friends shrugged. Howie laughed. "You cheer it up!"

Debbie Dadey and Marcia Thornton Jones have fun writing stories together. When they both worked at an elementary school in Lexington, Kentucky, Debbie was the school librarian and Marcia was a teacher. During their lunch break in the school cafeteria, they came up with the idea of the Bailey School kids.

Recently Debbie and her family moved to Aurora, Illinois. Marcia and her husband still live in Kentucky where she continues to teach. How do these authors still write together? They talk on the phone and use computers and fax machines!

Creepy, weird, wacky and
funny things happen to
the Bailey School Kids!™
Collect and read them all!

LITTLE 🍎 APPLE®

Here are some of our favorite Little Apples.

There are fun times ahead with kids just like you in Little Apple books! Once you take a bite out of a Little Apple—you'll want to read more!

Reading Excitement for Kids with BIG Appetites!

- [ ] NA45899-X **Amber Brown Is Not a Crayon**
  Paula Danziger $2.99
- [ ] NA93425-2 **Amber Brown Goes Fourth**
  Paula Danziger $2.99
- [ ] NA50207-7 **You Can't Eat Your Chicken Pox, Amber Brown**
  Paula Danziger $2.99
- [ ] NA42833-0 **Catwings** Ursula K. LeGuin $2.95
- [ ] NA42832-2 **Catwings Return** Ursula K. LeGuin $3.50
- [ ] NA41821-1 **Class Clown** Johanna Hurwitz $2.99
- [ ] NA42400-9 **Five True Horse Stories**
  Margaret Davidson $2.99
- [ ] NA43868-9 **The Haunting of Grade Three**
  Grace Maccarone $2.99
- [ ] NA40966-2 **Rent a Third Grader** B.B. Hiller $2.99
- [ ] NA41944-7 **The Return of the Third Grade Ghost Hunters**
  Grace Maccarone $2.99
- [ ] NA42031-3 **Teacher's Pet** Johanna Hurwitz $3.50

Available wherever you buy books...or use the coupon below.